CHAPTER 1:
BACK AGAIN!

One beautiful evening, in a peaceful meadow near a busy city, a cow chewed her cud.

The cow's name was Hillary. She was a lovely cow. But her cud was not lovely. Cud never is.

In case you don't know, cud is grass that a cow has chewed, swallowed, and then brought back up from its stomach to chew all over again. Disgusting? You bet.

But Hillary wasn't disgusted by her cud. She

thought it was delightful. She was enjoying her-self, standing in a meadow, chewing her delight-ful cud, when . . .

VWOOOM! An intense white light shone down on Hillary from above. "Moo?" she wondered. Then the cow looked up and saw something very strange: a bright yellow spaceship, shaped like a submarine! It had two eyes and two big teeth painted on it.

And it was coming down toward the meadow. Quickly.

Hillary's eyes bulged. She had no interest in sticking around to see who—or what—might come out of the spaceship. Quickly swallowing her cud (she could always bring it up again later), she ran out of the meadow to join her fellow cows. She decided to not tell them what she'd seen. She didn't want them to think she was crazy.

VWHOMP! The yellow spaceship landed on the grass. A door opened, and out ran . . . three Rabbids.

The spaceship zoomed away, leaving the three Rabbids behind.

Just in case you're not familiar with Rabbids, they look a little like Earth rabbits. But they're not rabbits, and they don't come from Earth. Rabbids are bigger than rabbits. And much, much more destructive. Some say Rabbids are going to take over our planet. Others say they're going to *destroy* our planet.

One of the Rabbids turned to the other two Rabbids. Making a sharp gesture with his hand, he said, "Bwah bwah BWAH!" and ran out of the meadow. Since the other two Rabbids followed him, it's possible he meant, "Follow *me*!" Or "Do what I do!" Or "I suggest we all run out of this meadow immediately!"

They hadn't run very far when they reached the edge of the brightly lit city. The front Rabbid saw something and stopped so suddenly that the other two Rabbids bumped into him. *THUNK!*

"Bwoooooh!" he cooed, his voice full of wonder.

He was staring at a fire hydrant.

The leader Rabbid raised his hand in greeting and said, "Bwah bwoh bweeeeh bwoh bwah bwah." Which might have meant "Take me to your leader." Or "Pleased to meet you." Or possibly, "Do you happen to speak Rabbid?"

The fire hydrant said nothing. It did not speak Rabbid. Or French. Or any other language. This fire hydrant, like all fire hydrants, didn't speak at all.

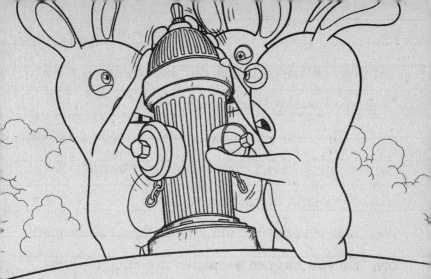

The Rabbid started to get annoyed with the silent fire hydrant. He waved his hand in front of it. He tapped it. Thumped it. Slapped it. Ouch. That hurt.

Finally the Rabbid grabbed the hydrant and gave a mighty twist. The other two Rabbids jumped in to help their leader. They twisted as hard as they could, until . . .

WHOOSH!!!

The hydrant shot a column of white water straight up into the sky.

And on top of that geyser was the leader

Rabbid. "BWAAAAAHHH!!!" he screamed as he rode the powerful jet of water.

At first the other two Rabbids didn't know where their leader had gone to. "Bwah?" they asked, looking around, puzzled.

Then one of them thought to look up and spotted the leader on top of the water, tumbling and sputtering. He pointed and laughed. "BWAH HA HA!" When the third Rabbid saw what the second Rabbid was pointing at, he laughed hysterically too.

While they were laughing, the leader fell off the tower of water, landing right on top of them. *THWUMP!!!*

The three Rabbids stood up with their eyes rolling around. Then they shook themselves off and then started running toward the heart of the city.

The fire hydrant just kept shooting water up into the sky. It didn't care that the Rabbids were back.

But soon, everyone else would. . . .

CHAPTER 2

Catch a Rabbid . . . or Else!

Agent Glyker sat in his crummy chair in his crummy office, staring at the dusty screen of his crummy computer.

He felt discouraged.

Sure, he loved being a secret agent, working at the SGAII-RD (the Secret Government Agency for the Investigation of Intruders-Rabbid Division). But if he didn't catch a Rabbid soon, he'd never get promoted.

In fact he was starting to think he might even get fired.

When he first started working at the SGAII-RD, he figured his job was safe no matter what he did because his boss, Director Stern, was also his uncle. If Uncle Jim fired him, Glyker's mom would be really mad at her brother. She might not even give him a birthday present. But Glyker was starting to worry. . . .

Just then Director Stern bellowed from his office, "GLYKER! GET IN HERE! NOW!"

Glyker ran down the hallway as fast as he could to the director's office. It was much bigger and nicer than Glyker's office. (But then, many boxes tossed in trash bins were nicer than Glyker's office.) "Yes, Uncle Jim?" he asked, peeking his head in through the doorway.

"DON'T CALL ME THAT!" roared Director Stern. "Now, tell me. What is our number one priority?"

12

Agent Glyker knew the answer since his boss had told him about a million times. "To catch a Rabbid," he said.

"And what will happen if we don't catch a Rabbid soon?" Director Stern asked.

Glyker had heard this many times too. He shifted his feet nervously. "Our funding will be cut, so we'll all be out of jobs."

The director nodded his head vigorously. "Exactly," he agreed. "So I want to make this very clear: If you don't catch a Rabbid within one week, you're fired!"

Glyker gulped. "But we haven't gotten a call about Rabbids in days! And Mom'll be so disappointed—"

"Don't try that 'Mom' stuff on me!" Director Stern yelled. "We'll get a call soon. I can feel it in my bones. Plus, I've got an idea to bring in more calls."

He proudly held up a piece of paper. It said "WANTED" across the top. In the middle was a drawing of a Rabbid. (Not a very good drawing. Director Stern wasn't much of an artist.) At the bottom was a phone number.

"You're putting our phone number on a poster?" Glyker asked, puzzled. "Aren't we supposed to be a *secret* agency?"

Stern frowned. "Never mind that. Here." He handed the paper to Glyker. "Make a thousand copies of this poster. Then put them up all over the city."

Glyker took the poster and studied it. "But how am I supposed to catch a Rabbid if I'm busy putting up posters?"

"That's your problem," Director Stern answered gruffly. "Remember: You've got one week to catch a Rabbid. Or you're *FIRED*!"

CHAPTER 3:

Playing in Traffic

On a beautiful, sunny afternoon, the three Rabbids were running through the city, cutting through backyards and stomping through flower beds. As they ran, they made noises, "Bwah bwah bwah bwaddlety bwah ha ha!" It was hard to tell if they were laughing or singing. Maybe they were doing both.

They were dashing along a smooth cement sidewalk when they came upon an intersection near a school. A crossing guard (a nice elderly man named Mr. Twinpeppers) held out an orange flag as he helped two young students cross the street. Cars stopped when he held out his flag.

"Bwah?" said the Rabbid who seemed to be the trio's leader, confused by what he was seeing.

"Bye, kids!" Mr. Twinpeppers said. "See you tomorrow!"

"Bye, Mr. Twinpeppers!" said the two kids as they hurried home.

The Rabbids watched all this, fascinated. They

hurried over to Mr. Twinpeppers's corner and stayed behind him so he wouldn't notice them.

"Well, that's the last of 'em," Mr. Twinpeppers said to himself. "Guess I'll head home to feed Habanero."

19

He set down his flag, folded up his chair, and put it in the trunk of his car.

When he turned around, his flag was gone.

"Where'd my flag go?" he wondered. "It was here just a second ago . . ."

20

Mr. Twinpeppers looked around, scratching his head. No flag.

He was in a hurry to get home and feed his Chihuahua, Habanero, so he decided he'd just make another flag. He liked projects, anyway.

21

Whistling, he got into his car and then drove off.

Behind a nearby bush, there was a bullfight going on.

Well, not a bullfight exactly. More of a Rabbid fight.

The Rabbids weren't mad at one another, though. They were having a great time. Their leader was holding the crossing guard's flag out at his side and shaking it. Then one of the other two Rabbids would put his head down, snort, and charge at the flag like a raging bull. At the last second, the leader would whip the flag out of the way, and the bull-Rabbid would run past.

Then all three would laugh: "BWAH HA HA HA HA!!!"

Soon, though, one of the bull-Rabbids wanted to take a turn as the matador-Rabbid. He tried to grab the flag, but the leader ran away, waving the flag.

The leader Rabbid ran right out into the street. And a car was headed straight toward him! He saw the car coming at him and froze, just staring at the car.

EERRRRRRRGHK!

The car slammed on its brakes and stopped just in time.

"Bwhew!" The Rabbid sighed. Then he looked at his flag. Had this thing made the car stop?

The Rabbid stepped aside and waved his orange flag as if to say, "Please go ahead."

And the car did!

The Rabbid's eyes widened. This thing (the flag, though he didn't know that word) could control cars! (Actually, the Rabbid didn't know the word "car," either. He thought of them as big metal ground spaceships that never managed to take off and fly.)

As his two fellow Rabbids joined him on the other side of the street, the leader smiled. Just think what they could *do* with this thing. . . .

He waited for another car to come along. But the school was on a quiet street, so there weren't a lot of cars. The leader grew impatient. They needed to go where there were *lots* of cars. . . .

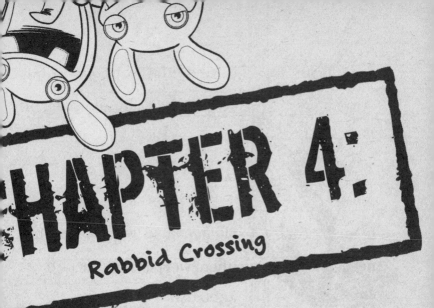

CHAPTER 4:
Rabbid Crossing

Agent Glyker was sweating. He'd spent the whole afternoon putting up posters. It was harder work than it looked.

KA-CHUNK! He stapled yet another "WANTED" poster to yet another telephone pole. He sighed and looked at the poster. It was crooked. Oh well. At least he hadn't gotten a splinter this time.

"Is there a reward?"

Glyker turned around. A kid was standing right

behind him eating a candy bar. He had chocolate on his face.

"What?" Glyker asked.

"Is there a reward?" the kid repeated with his mouth full. "For spotting one of those Rabbids?"

Glyker shook his head. Director Stern hadn't said anything about a reward. "The only reward," he explained, "is knowing you've done the right thing for planet Earth. After all, we're under invasion here."

The kid frowned. "There should be a reward. Cash. A motorcycle. Or maybe a trip to Hawaii."

Glyker put away his stapler and then picked up his heavy backpack. "Look, kid, I've got a lot of posters to put up, so if you'll excuse me—"

"Don't you want to know where I saw one?" the kid asked.

Glyker paused. "Saw one what?"

"Rabbid," said the kid. "In fact, I saw three of 'em. Today."

Agent Glyker was excited. Maybe he wouldn't be fired after all! "Where?" he asked eagerly. "Where'd you see the Rabbids?"

The boy folded his arms across his chest stubbornly. "There oughta be a reward."

Glyker remembered something: a candy bar in his backpack! He'd been saving it for a late afternoon snack. He quickly dug through the backpack, pulled out the candy bar, and held it up. "Just tell me where you saw the Rabbids, and it's all yours."

The kid squinted. "One lousy candy bar?" He considered it. "Okay. They're downtown. At the corner of First and Main."

Glyker tossed the candy bar to the kid and jumped into his car. "Thanks!" he called as he sped off.

The kid looked at his reward and shook his head. "I don't even like this kind of candy bar," he muttered to himself.

As Glyker approached downtown in his beat-up old car, he started to hear honking and yelling. Soon all the cars came to a complete stop. There was a huge traffic jam. A helicopter from the local news station buzzed overhead.

Could this have anything to do with the Rabbids? Glyker wondered.

Yes. Yes, it could.

Glyker pulled his car over to the curb and parked. Then he jumped out of his car and ran toward the corner of First and Main.

31

From half a block away, he saw them.

Three Rabbids were standing in the middle of the intersection. One of the Rabbids was waving a crossing guard's orange flag, directing traffic. The other two were whistling and pointing at cars, telling them where to go.

But the Rabbids were sending the cars in all the

wrong directions. They sent them the wrong way down a one-way street. They sent them into a dead-end alley. They even sent them onto the sidewalk! Taxis and buses were blasting their horns, and pedestrians were running into stores to hide.

The only ones having a great time were the Rabbids, who kept laughing hysterically. "BWHAH HA HA HA HA!!!"

Agent Glyker wasted no time. Holding up his SGAII-RD badge, he ran toward the intersection, yelling, "STOP!"

He really shouldn't have yelled, because the Rabbids spotted him coming. They quickly started to leave, but first the leader couldn't resist directing a couple more cars into the intersection.

The cars headed straight at Glyker!

At the last second, Glyker dove out of the way. The two drivers swerved their cars, narrowly missing a collision.

When Glyker looked up, the Rabbids had disappeared.

What are the Rabbids up to now?

Glyker thought frantically. *Are they trying to ruin our transportation system? Is this all part of their invasion? And where will the Rabbids strike next?*

CHAPTER 5:
Where They Struck Next

The Rabbids had run away from the intersection of First and Main as fast as their stumpy legs would carry them—which was surprisingly fast.

But when they looked around, they didn't see anyone chasing them, so they slowed down.

And when they slowed down, they noticed a very interesting place.

From inside the building in front of them came the sounds of babies playing. When the Rabbids looked through the windows, they saw lots of babies crawling around and playing with toys.

It was a daycare center.

But to the Rabbids, it just looked like *fun!*

The three Rabbids hurried into the daycare center. The leader walked up to a baby playing with blocks on the floor.

"Bwah bwoh bwah!" said the leader, raising his hand in greeting.

"Goo goo gah!" said the baby. It reached out to grab the Rabbid, but the leader backed away quickly. He didn't want to be grabbed.

The baby crawled away. He lay down on a mat and soon fell asleep.

It must have been nap time for everyone at the center, because the other babies were falling asleep too.

But the Rabbids didn't feel like taking a nap. They wanted to have *fun*!

They messed around with the baby blocks for a while, but the blocks made terrible hats. And shoes. And chairs. Boring. . . .

Poking around in a back room, one of the Rabbids found something very interesting: a bin full of used diapers!

"Bwah ha!" he said, pulling one of the stinky diapers out of the bin.

One of the other Rabbids was thinking about yelling at the babies to wake them up, when . . .

THWAP!

Something hit him in the back of the head. He whirled around and found a smelly, leaky used diaper on the floor.

"BWAH HA HA HA HA!" The Rabbid who'd thrown the diaper laughed.

The Rabbid who'd been hit with the diaper picked it up, and flung it back at his friend. Soon the three Rabbids were positioned around the day-care center whipping used diapers at one another.

THWAP!

SPLORP!

SPLAT!

The adults in charge of watching the babies had settled into chairs with magazines as soon as the babies had fallen asleep. They loved nap time, since it gave them a little break. Concentrating on articles about pop stars and health tips, they hadn't noticed the Rabbids.

Until the diapers started flying.

The adults looked up from their magazines. One of them said, "What the heck is going on?"

A woman who'd been reading an article about Rabbids invading planet Earth immediately recognized the white creatures who were tossing diapers at one another. "WE'RE BEING INVADED!" she screamed.

CHAPTER 6:

A Deluge of Diapers

Agent Glyker pulled up in front of the daycare center and jumped out of his car. Several daycare workers were standing in the front yard, holding babies in their arms.

Glyker hurried up to the workers, flashing his badge to identify himself. "Thank goodness you're here!" cried the woman who'd screamed about an invasion. "We got all the babies out safely, but those awful Rabbids are still inside."

"That's great!" Glyker said, grinning. Maybe he wouldn't be fired after all! That promotion was as good as his.

Then he noticed all the workers frowning at him. They didn't think it was "great" that their daycare center had been invaded by maniacal Rabbids.

45

Glyker put on a serious face. "I mean it's great you got all the babies out safely." He headed toward the front door. "Just leave these Rabbids to me." Then he grabbed the knob to fling the door open dramatically.

Except it was locked.

"Oops," another woman apologized.

46

"Sorry. We forgot to tell you we locked them in."

"Good thinking," Glyker assured her as she took out a key and unlocked the door. "We don't want these Rabbids going anywhere."

Glyker flung open the door and leaped inside, ready for anything.

Nothing happened.

It was quiet inside the daycare center. Extremely stinky, but quiet. He saw several used diapers on the floor, but no Rabbids.

Where were they? Had they gone out the back door? Or a window? Agent Glyker stood in the middle of the room, thinking about his next move.

THWAP!!!

A used diaper hit Glyker squarely in
the head and slid down his back.

"BWAH HA HA HA HA HA!!!"

Glyker whipped around and spotted a Rabbid standing in a doorway leading to another room. The Rabbid was laughing. At Glyker. Hard. In fact, the Rabbid was laughing as though he'd never seen anything so funny in his whole life.

Glyker didn't like being hit with a used diaper. He *really* didn't like being laughed at. Feeling *really* mad, he ran toward the Rabbid. The Rabbid took off to the other room. As soon as Glyker crossed through the doorway . . .

THWAP! THWAP!

The two other Rabbids nailed him right in the

face with a couple more used diapers.

"BWAH HA HA HA HA!!!"

For a second, Glyker couldn't see. He wiped the diapers (and their contents) off his face, blinked and looked for the Rabbids. They were heading through a door into a small kitchen.

"Halt!" he yelled. He doubted it would do much good, but it made him feel more official.

Careful not to slip on any diapers, Glyker sprinted into the kitchen. The three Rabbids were standing on the other side of the room. They didn't have any diapers in their hands, but one of them was holding a rope.

Glyker smiled. "Now I've got you," he gloated.

Then one of the Rabbids pointed up, right above Glyker's head. "Oh right," Glyker said. "Like I'm going to look up. Oldest trick in the book!"

The Rabbid shrugged and yanked on the rope. *SHABLORP-BLOP-BLOP-BLORP!* Hundreds of used diapers fell on Agent Glyker, burying him in a stinky pile.

As he dug his way out of the diaper pile, Glyker saw the last Rabbid disappearing through an open window. He looked back at Glyker, grinned, and waggled his butt.

By the time Glyker ran out the back door, they were gone.

"*Now the Rabbids are going after our children. This is serious!*" he thought. "*Also, I seriously need a bath.*"

CHAPTER 7:

Bubbles!

The next day the Rabbids found themselves in a wonderful place full of flowers, bushes, and beautiful trees. They didn't know it, but it was the city's biggest park.

But the Rabbids weren't interested in flowers, bushes, and beautiful trees. They'd seen all those things before.

"Bwhaaah." One of the Rabbids yawned, bored.

They wanted to see something new. Something they'd never seen before. Something like . . . that! A big bubble, glistening with a rainbow of colors, floated by!

"Bwoooooh!" said the Rabbids as they watched the bubble rise on the wind.

POP! The bubble hit the branch of a maple tree.

"Bwaaah." The Rabbids moaned, disappointed. They looked around to see if another bubble would float by.

"Bwah!" shouted one of the Rabbids, pointing. Another bubble! The Rabbids jumped as high as they could, trying to catch the wonderful see-through ball.

POP! This time the bubble popped without even touching anything. "Bwaah." The three Rabbids sighed.

Then one of the Rabbids got an idea. "Bwah bwah!" he cried, motioning for his two fellow invaders to follow him.

The idea the Rabbid had gotten was this:
Maybe if they went back in the opposite direction
the bubble had been floating, they'd find out
where it had come from.

The idea worked splendidly.

As the Rabbids pushed through
a row of bushes, they saw

something wonderful. Something miraculous!

At a birthday party, a young man was showing kids how to make all kinds of bubbles. He had a plastic wading pool full of bubble solution. He also had a bucket full of wands to dip into the pool and then wave through the air.

"See," he said, "with this hoop I can make a really *big* bubble!"

And he did. The Rabbids watched, amazed. Then they ran forward. . . .

It was a good thing Agent Glyker had put up several of Director Stern's posters in the park. One of the moms at the bubble party called the number on the poster immediately. But she was too upset to give very good information.

"RABBIDS! HERE! AT THE PARK! RUINING OUR BIRTHDAY PARTY! INVASION!!!" she screamed into her phone.

Glyker held the old-fashioned phone in his office farther away from his ear.

"Which park?" he asked. "You mean the big park in the center of the city?"

"YES!" the mom shouted. "HURRY!"

CHAPTER 8:

To the Park!

Agent Glyker got to the park as fast as he could. Once there, he quickly found the site of the ruined bubble party.

It wasn't pretty.

All the little kids were huddling under a tree with their parents and the Bubble Guy, watching the Rabbids.

Two of the Rabbids were using bubble paddles like tennis rackets, batting a bow from a birthday

present back and forth. When they got tired of this,
they went back to tearing open all the presents.

"Those are *my* presents!" wailed a little boy.

The leader Rabbid picked up the pool of bubble
solution and drank it all. Then he started belching
huge bubbles.

BUUUURRRPP!

"My bubble solution!" protested the Bubble Guy.

Agent Glyker had learned his lesson about yelling at the Rabbids to stop. He decided to sneak up on them, hoping to grab at least one of them.

But the Rabbids spotted Glyker creeping toward them. They seemed to recognize him from the daycare center. They pointed and laughed.

"BWAH HA HA HA HA!"

As the leader laughed, streams of bubbles poured from his wide-open mouth.

As soon as he realized he'd been spotted, Glyker started running toward the Rabbids.

But they took off running too. And they were faster than Glyker.

Glyker ran up to a guy who was renting bikes. He flashed his badge, shouted "Official intruder investigation!" jumped on a bike, and pedaled away.

"Hey!" yelled the guy. "You've got to pay for that!"

"I'll bring it back!" Glyker called back over his shoulder.

"You're supposed to bring it back *and* pay for it!" the guy shouted.

The Rabbids saw that Glyker was gaining on

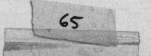

them now that he had a bike. Where could they go that no bike could go?

"Bwah ha!" said the leader, spotting the small lake in the middle of the park. (A few bubbles came out of his mouth as he spoke.) He led the other two Rabbids out onto a paddleboat. At first they weren't sure how to make it go, but then they saw a couple in another boat, pedaling with their feet.

"BWAH!" shouted the leader, pointing at the boat's pedals. The other two Rabbids got to work pedaling.

"Hey!" yelled the guy in charge of the boats. "You've got to pay for that!"

Glyker rode up on the bike, jumped off, and leaped into a paddleboat. He started pedaling like mad to catch up with the Rabbids.

"Hey!" yelled the boat guy again. "What is this? Free day?"

"Yay!" said a nearby kid. "It's free day!" He tried to climb into a paddleboat, but the boat guy stopped him.

Glyker was getting closer to the Rabbids.

"BWAH BWAH!" shouted the leader as though he were saying "FASTER!" The other two Rabbids started pedaling even faster.

Even though his legs were starting to ache, Glyker pedaled as fast as he could. His paddleboat churned through the water, kicking up waves. He was gaining on the Rabbids again. They were headed toward the grassy edge of the lake. Were they going to jump out and run?

The leader turned around and faced Glyker. *"BUUURRRPP!"* he roared, belching out a huge bubble.

The bubble blew right into Glyker's face and popped. "Eww!" Glyker said. The bubble smelled horrible!

Distracted by the stinky bubble, Glyker swerved, pedaling his boat right into the shallow mud near the shore. *SHPLOOMPF!* He tried turning the pedals, but they wouldn't budge. He was stuck!

As he helplessly watched the Rabbids pedal away in their boat, he saw the leader wave at him.

"Bwah bwah!" he called back to Glyker.

The other two Rabbids laughed. The secret agent growled in frustration. He had a feeling his boss wasn't going to be very happy when he heard about this.

CHAPTER 9:
The Boss Isn't Happy

SHPLORP. SHPLUMPF. SHPLORP. SHPLUMPF.

Agent Glyker trudged down the hallway to his crummy little office, leaving a trail of mud prints on the floor. He hoped Director Stern hadn't heard him coming in.

No such luck.

"GLYKER!" bellowed Director Stern from his much nicer office. "GET IN HERE!"

Glyker sighed and headed down the hallway to

his boss's office, trying to wipe all the smelly lake mud off his shoes before he got there.

When Glyker stepped meekly into the office, Stern glared at him. "So," Stern said, "I see muddy shoes. I see an agent who's in serious danger of being fired. But I don't see a Rabbid."

"No, sir," Agent Glyker admitted. "But I was really close. I almost had one."

"Yeah?" Director Stern sneered. "Well, 'almost had one' equals 'almost fired'! Did you put up those posters?"

Glyker nodded eagerly. "Yes, sir! Every one! In fact, our last call was in response to—"

BRRRRING! The boss's phone rang. "Yeah?" he answered gruffly. But then, as he listened to the caller, he started to nod and smile. "That's great. Thank you. We'll be right there."

He hung up. "Another Rabbid sighting. At the concert hall. The orchestra's playing tonight, and the mayor himself will be there."

"I'm on it!" Agent Glyker said, turning to go.

"Hold it," Director Stern said, standing up. "I don't want you messing this up. I'm coming with you."

Glyker gulped. "Yes, sir," he said.

CHAPTER 10

Concert Chaos

Agent Glyker and Director Stern jumped out of Glyker's car and hurried up to the front doors of the concert hall. The hall's manager was waiting for them, nervously pacing and wringing his hands.

"Thank goodness you're here!" he cried. "It's terrible! Rabbids! In my concert hall! And the mayor is here tonight!"

Director Stern put up both hands and made

a calming gesture. "Okay, okay, relax," he reassured the manager. "Everything's going to be fine. Now, where are the Rabbids?"

The manager threw his hands up in the air. "Who knows?! All I know is two of our patrons said they saw three Rabbids entering the hall just before the concert started."

Stern looked very determined. "We'll find them," he promised.

"Come on," he said to Glyker, heading into the concert hall.

But the manager stopped the two investigators before they opened the fancy gold doors. "The concert's already started! You'll have to do this very quietly!"

Agent Glyker patted the manager's shoulder reassuringly. "Don't worry," he said. "We're secret agents. Quiet is our specialty."

Director Stern and Agent Glyker slipped into the back of the concert hall as silently as possible. Onstage, the city's symphony orchestra was playing a slow piece of classical music.

Glyker and Stern stared hard, searching for Rabbids. But they didn't see any. The concert seemed to be going smoothly.

"Maybe this was a false alarm," Stern whispered.

Then . . . *SQUEAK!* In the middle of a quiet passage featuring the violins, a clarinet squeaked loudly. The audience murmured. *SQUEAK! SQUEAK!*

The conductor scowled. Had the clarinetist made a horrible, loud mistake?

Glyker pointed at the back of the symphony. "There!" he hissed. A Rabbid was strolling offstage. And he was carrying a clarinet, twirling it like a baton.

"Should I jump onstage and make an announcement?" Glyker asked. "If we stop the concert and have the ushers guard the doors, we can catch them for sure!"

As Glyker headed down the aisle toward the stage, Stern grabbed his arm.

"Forget it!" Stern whispered, pulling him back. Annoyed music-lovers turned and glared at them.

At the back of the hall, Stern whispered, "I don't want to panic everyone and start a stampede. Also, I don't want to ruin this concert for the mayor. He *loves* classical music!"

Other loud sounds started to pop out of the orchestra: cymbals, tambourines, and gongs. The Rabbids had found the percussion section.

Stern and Glyker ran as quickly (and as quietly) as they could to get to the stage. They hoped they could corner the Rabbids without ruining the concert.

From backstage, the secret agent and his boss could see the Rabbids poking around in the percussionists' equipment. One of the Rabbids picked

up a triangle and threw it like a ninja star. It flew across the stage and landed—*KLANG!*—on the wooden floor.

A percussionist saw this and fumed with fury, but kept playing.

Another Rabbid found a pair of drumsticks and stuck them in his mouth. Then he did his best imitation of a walrus.

83

Glyker and Stern snuck behind the back curtain to get closer to the Rabbids. . . .

The third Rabbid found a cymbal. Delighted, he put it on his head to wear as a hat.

By the time Glyker and Stern reached the other side of the stage, the Rabbids had disappeared.

Where were they?

Glyker looked around desperately. Then he spotted them. The three Rabbids were climbing up a ladder that went all the way up to the top of the concert hall.

He pointed and hissed, "There!" Director Stern grinned. "Now we've got 'em," he said. "Come on—let's use the ladder!"

As the concert continued far below, Glyker and Stern climbed the ladder way up into the space where the long velvet curtains hung over the stage. Above them, they could see the three Rabbids quickly climbing all the way up to the ceiling.

84

When they reached the top, the Rabbids pushed open a trap-door and climbed through it. For a moment, Glyker and Stern could see the stars in the night sky.

Then the trapdoor shut. **CLANG!**

CHAPTER 11:
Up on the Roof

"Push harder!" Director Stern growled. Agent Glyker was trying to push the trapdoor open, but it seemed to be stuck.

Actually, it wasn't just stuck. On the other side, the three Rabbids were sitting on it.

But then one of them noticed something interesting on the roof of the concert hall. It was the opening of an air shaft, but to the Rabbid, it looked like a huge musical instrument.

"Bwoooh!" the Rabbid said, jumping off the hatch to go investigate. His two fellow Rabbids jumped off to follow him.

When he reached the air shaft, the Rabbid yelled, "BWAAAHHH!!!" into it. Far below, in the concert hall, the conductor scowled as a loud "BWAH" interrupted the symphony. The mayor looked at his wife, puzzled.

CLANK! Glyker finally managed to shove open the trapdoor. He and Stern hurried up through it.

There was a full moon, so they could easily see everything on the roof: air shafts, air-conditioning units, and a bucket someone had left behind . . .

But no Rabbids.

Then Agent Glyker pointed silently. There was one Rabbid on one side of the roof and another on the other side, near the edge.

Director Stern nodded. He understood that Glyker thought they should each run and grab one of the Rabbids.

Without saying anything, Glyker and Stern ran toward the Rabbids. The Rabbids spotted them coming and yelled.

"BWWAAAAAHHHH!!!"

Agent Glyker (who was younger and quicker than Stern) got to his Rabbid first. He dove and

grabbed the Rabbid around the waist. The Rabbid yelled and squirmed, but Glyker held on tight.

"Got him!" Glyker yelled.

"HELP!!!" Stern answered.

Glyker looked over toward his boss. He was hanging onto a railing with his feet dangling over the edge of the roof!

When Stern had run toward the other Rabbid, the creature had leaped out of the way at the last second, and Stern hadn't been able to stop himself. He'd almost fallen off the roof! Now he was grasping the railing, but he wasn't sure how much longer he could hold on. . . .

Agent Glyker didn't hesitate for a second. He let the Rabbid go, ran over to his boss, and tugged him back up onto the roof.

When they looked around, a yellow spaceship, shaped like a submarine, was landing on the other side of the roof. The three Rabbids ran into it. Just before they went inside, all three waggled their butts at Glyker and Stern.

"No!" Agent Glyker yelled. "Stop!" But he knew they wouldn't.

FWOOOOM!!! The spaceship zoomed up into the night sky and disappeared.

Glyker shook his head. He knew what this meant: no Rabbid, no job.

"So," he finally said, "I guess I'm fired."

Director Stern looked at him for a moment. Then he asked, "What's your job title again?"

Puzzled, Glyker said, "Secret Agent, Third Class."

"Well, starting tomorrow," Stern said, "you're Secret Agent, Second Class."

"A promotion!" Glyker said, grinning. "Thanks, Uncle Jim!"

"DON'T CALL ME THAT!" roared Director Stern.

Glyker's To-Do List:

1. Tell Mom about promotion.

2. Remind Mom that chocolate cake is my favorite.

3. Buy stain remover.

4. Find source of mysterious smell in refrigerator.

5. Send Uncle Jim a thank-you card to thank him for promotion?

ATTENTION !!!